YO-KAI WATCH™ Epic Showdowns

Over **20** face-offs you've never seen!

By Meredith Rusu

© LEVEL-5/YWP. Produced by Scholastic Inc. under license from LEVEL-5.

Published by Scholastic Inc., *Publishers since 1920.* SCHOLASTIC and associated logos are trademarks and/or registered trademarks of Scholastic Inc.

The publisher does not have any control over and does not assume any responsibility for author or third-party websites or their content.

No part of this publication may be reproduced, stored in a retrieval system, or transmitted in any form or by any means, electronic, mechanical, photocopying, recording, or otherwise, without written permission of the publisher. For information regarding permission, write to Scholastic Inc., Attention: Permissions Department, 557 Broadway, New York, NY 10012.

This book is a work of fiction. Names, characters, places, and incidents are either the product of the author's imagination or are used fictitiously, and any resemblance to actual persons, living or dead, business establishments, events, or locales is entirely coincidental.

ISBN 978-1-338-05461-3

10 9 8 7 6 5 4 3 2 1   16 17 18 19 20

Printed in the U.S.A.   40

First printing 2016

Cover design by Angela Jun and Becky James
Interior design by Angela Jun and Kay Petronio

SCHOLASTIC INC.

W9-BLG-695

IT'S SHOWDOWN TIME!

Have you ever wondered who would win in a battle between . . .

JIBANYAN VS. MANJIMUTT

Now's your chance to find out!

Strap on your Yo-kai Watch and get your Yo-kai Medals ready . . . it's time for your favorite Yo-kai to go head-to-head!

For each battle, you'll get all the stats and facts you need to decide which Yo-kai should be victorious. Then check out the final rulings on the last page to see if you're a Yo-kai expert!

CHARMING

JIBANYAN

Jibanyan used to be a real cat . . . until a mishap with a truck made him a real Yo-kai. Now he's determined to take revenge on unsuspecting cars using his Paws of Fury! Jibanyan's secret weapon is his adorable penchant for slacking off.

STATS

Tribe: Charming

Attack: Sharp Claws

Soultimate Move: Paws of Fury

Favorite Food: Seafood and chocobars

Secret Weapon: Adorable penchant for slacking off

Inspirit: Slow Down

Easiness to Befriend: ★ ★ ★

THE SHOWDOWN

Jibanyan unleashes Paws of Fury, but Manjimutt disarms him with a depressing heart-to-heart. Both Yo-kai have sad backstories. Will this matchup end in flying fists or tearful hugs?

EERIE

STATS

Tribe: Eerie

Attack: Chomp

Soultimate Move: Creepy Superbite

Favorite Food: Chinese food

Secret Weapon: Making you share his misery

Inspirit: Confusion

Easiness to Befriend: ★★★★★

MANJIMUTT

Poor Manjimutt. He's neither a man nor an adorable puppy: he's a sad mix of the two, with a self-worth complex to boot. But behind that downtrodden expression is the soul of a dreamer. He may just worm his way into your heart . . . or make you pity him enough to let him win.

BLAZION VS. WALKAPPA

BRAVE

BLAZION

Two words describe this fiery Yo-kai: PUMPED UP. Blazion fills people with red-hot enthusiasm and accepts nothing less than victory. He's not interested in your backstory. He's not even interested in your name. He just wants to know one thing: Are you ready to GO!?

STATS

Tribe: Brave

Attack: Practiced Punch

Soultimate Move: Blazing Fist

Favorite Food: Meat

Secret Weapon: Seemingly endless energy

Inspirit: Emblaze

Easiness to Befriend: ★★★★

THE SHOWDOWN

Fire versus water: a formidable matchup. Blazion comes charging at Walkappa with fists blazing. But will Walkappa's go-with-the-flow attitude rain on Blazion's firestorm parade?

♥ CHARMING

STATS

Tribe: Charming

Attack: Punch

Soultimate Move: Mega Waterfall

Favorite Food: Vegetables

Secret Weapon: Convincing his opponents to just chill out

Inspirit: Nap Time

Easiness to Befriend: ★ ★ ★

WALKAPPA

Walkappa's a pretty laid-back dude. While most kappas prefer to stay in the water, Walkappa walks around and pours water on his head to keep his plate wet. This Yo-kai is slick at defusing confrontations. But his one weakness is his head plate. If it goes dry, he's toast.

ROUGHRAFF VS. HAPPIERRE

TOUGH

STATS

ROUGHRAFF

Roughraff is Yo-kai Public Enemy Number One—and proud of it! This rebel makes good kids go bad and is responsible for 98% of the troublemakers worldwide. Roughraff handles Yo-kai battles the same way—he's bad to the bone.

Tribe: Tough

Attack: Headbutt

Soultimate Move: Staredown

Favorite Food: Ramen

Secret Weapon: Smack talk

Inspirit: Rebel Soul

Easiness to Befriend: ★ ★ ★ ★

It's Roughraff's tough-guy act against Happierre's tough love. One's smug, the other's all hug. Will Roughraff bring Happierre to the dark side? Or will Happierre turn Roughraff's frown upside down?

HEARTFUL

STATS

Tribe: Heartful

Attack: Body Bash

Soultimate Move: Air of Happiness

Favorite Food: Bread

Secret Weapon: Hugging it out

Inspirit: Cheerfulness

Easiness to Befriend: ★ ★ ★ ☆

HAPPIERRE

This cheery Yo-kai emanates warmth and happiness wherever he goes. In battle, he crushes his opponents with kindness! Happierre removes all the tension in the air and cheers up even the most aggressive Yo-kai. He's known to stop the fight before it even begins.

CHARMING

KOMASAN

This harmless country bumpkin is a big softie with a weakness for ice cream. He'd rather write home to Mama about his adventures in the big city than fight with anyone. Still, given the right circumstances, Komasan has what it takes to duke it out.

STATS

Tribe: Charming

Attack: Punch

Soultimate Move: Spirit Dance

Favorite Food: Milk

Secret Weapon: His disarming country accent

Inspirit: Burn

Easiness to Befriend: ★ ★ ★

THE SHOWDOWN

Oh my swirls, it's brother versus brother! This showdown seems likely to end with ice cream in the park. But who do you think would triumph in a battle of the brothers?

CHARMING

STATS

Tribe: Charming

Attack: Punch

Soultimate Move: Wild Zaps

Favorite Food: Milk

Secret Weapon: Spunk

Inspirit: Tiger Power

Easiness to Befriend: ★★★★

KOMAJIRO

Komajiro is Komasan's little brother, and he admires his big bro more than anyone in the whole wide Yo-kai world! This spunky little guy has a big heart and wants to learn all about life in the city. Komajiro will do whatever it takes to impress his older brother.

TATTLETELL VS. HIDABAT

MYSTERIOUS

STATS

TATTLETELL

Knowledge is power when it comes to Tattletell's attack strategy. She'll cling to her opponent's face and force them to reveal their secret weaknesses. Sometimes the worst thing she makes you reveal is that you love girl groups like Next HarMEOWny. But hey, who said shame isn't a weakness?

Tribe: Mysterious
Attack: Slap
Soultimate Move: Loving Slap
Favorite Food: Ramen
Secret Weapon: Spilling secrets
Inspirit: Disclose
Easiness to Befriend: ★ ★ ★

THE SHOWDOWN

Two unlikely opponents: one who tells all, and one who would rather say nothing. Tattletell may be able to get Hidabat to confess all his secrets, but Hidabat can be a difficult Yo-kai to catch hold of. Who will win?

SHADY

STATS

Tribe: Shady

Attack: Slap

Soultimate Move: Hidabat Harmony

Favorite Food: Meat

Secret Weapon: His vanishing act

Inspirit: Shut Away

Easiness to Befriend: ★★★★

HIDABAT

Hidabat is a Yo-kai that lurks in the shadows, possessing people and convincing them to lock themselves away from the rest of the world. He's not an easy Yo-kai to negotiate with . . . especially when it comes to going outside. But deep down, this shy guy is really just afraid of his own shadow.

BLIZZARIA VS. EVERFORE

❤️ **CHARMING**

STATS

BLIZZARIA

Things turn frosty when Blizzaria comes out to play. She's the evolved form of Frostina, and she can fully control her chilling power, making snow fall in summer and volcanoes freeze over. This serves her well in battle. She can freeze her opponents in their tracks!

Tribe: Charming

Attack: Smack Down

Soultimate Move: Shiny Snowdrifts

Favorite Food: Candy

Secret Weapon: Frostbite

Inspirit: Numbify

Easiness to Befriend: Unknown

THE SHOWDOWN

Blizzaria storms against Everfore with all her frosty might, but the wintry Yo-kai is just Everfore's type. Will Blizzaria leave Everfore frozen in time, or find that time is not on her side?

EERIE

STATS

Tribe: Eerie

Attack: Beat

Soultimate Move: Beauty Beam

Favorite Food: Milk

Secret Weapon: The best anti-aging cream on the market

Inspirit: Youth Drain

Easiness to Befriend: Unknown

EVERFORE

Everfore would just *love* to face off against you, especially if you're young and good-looking! This soul-sapping Yo-kai is the evolved form of Grumples. She sustains her own youth and beauty by absorbing it from others. Battling Everfore could take years off your life . . . literally!

EERIE

STATS

INSOMNI

Insomni is the stuff of nightmares. She enjoys keeping people awake all night so they fall asleep during the day . . . that is, unless she decides to give you her *undivided* attention. Then she won't let you fall asleep until she's bored with you . . . or you're almost dead.

Tribe: Eerie

Attack: Smack Down

Soultimate Move: Never Sleep Ever

Favorite Food: Candy

Secret Weapon: Nightmares

Inspirit: Insomnia

Easiness to Befriend: ★ ★ ★

THE SHOWDOWN

Insomni plans to keep Wiglin up all night, but that's just fine with the can't-stop, won't-stop bopping Yo-kai. Will sweet moves triumph over sweet dreams?

HEARTFUL

STATS

Tribe: Heartful

Attack: Slap

Soultimate Move: Wiggling Wave

Favorite Food: Ramen

Secret Weapon: Raisin' the Roof

Inspirit: Healthy Wakame

Easiness to Befriend: ★ ★ ★

WIGLIN

Wiglin has one goal in life: to dance all day and night! This seaweed Yo-kai wants to spread his hometown dance to the world. He may not have the heart of a fighter, but he's an expert at using his wiggling ways to dodge attacks.

KYUBI VS. CASANUVA

9
MYSTERIOUS

STATS

KYUBI

Kyubi is an elite master of fire who can make volcanoes erupt. But that's nothing compared to his heart-stealing ways. This nine-tailed fox enjoys transforming into a human so he can capture women's affection. In battle, you'll find yourself either smitten or scorched!

Tribe: Mysterious
Attack: Tail Slap
Soultimate Move: Inferno
Favorite Food: Seafood
Secret Weapon: His smoldering charm
Inspirit: Burn
Easiness to Befriend: Unknown

THE SHOWDOWN

Hearts are on fire in this red-hot showdown! Kyubi uses Inferno against Casanuva, but how can you defeat an opponent with so many ladies lining up to shield him?

MYSTERIOUS

STATS

Tribe: Mysterious

Attack: Guns Blazing

Soultimate Move: Heavenly Heart

Favorite Food: Bread

Secret Weapon: He wears his heart-cannon on his sleeve

Inspirit: Popularize

Easiness to Befriend: ★★★

CASANUVA

Casanuva is quite the charmer. He makes every lady he sees fall in love with him. His double-fisted heart cannons make him a powerful opponent—provided he can pull himself away from the mirror long enough to battle.

SIGNIBBLE VS. CHATALIE

MYSTERIOUS

SIGNIBBLE

Signibble likes to zap his opponents before the fight even begins. This sparky Yo-kai can manipulate electricity and uses his ability to make mischief wherever he goes. Whether he's changing your TV channel or making your hair stand on end, Signibble gives quite the shock!

STATS

Tribe: Mysterious

Attack: One-Two Punch

Soultimate Move: Signal Shock

Favorite Food: Rice balls

Secret Weapon: Lightning strikes

Inspirit: Paralyze

Easiness to Befriend: ★★★★

THE SHOWDOWN

Chatalie shoots Signibble with her inspiriting pink cell phone, but Signibble zaps her with a dose of Signal Shock. Will the charge be enough to change Chatalie's tune?

EERIE

STATS

Tribe: Eerie

Attack: Bite

Soultimate Move: Big Mouth

Favorite Food: Bread

Secret Weapon: Her pink cell phone

Inspirit: All Talk

Easiness to Befriend: ★ ★ ★ ★

CHATALIE

Chatterbox Chatalie just can't stop talking. She turns people into big mouths who break their promises, and Yo-kai into opponents who are all talk but no action. But don't blame her if you lose. She sure thinks it's something to brag about!

HEARTFUL

ENERFLY

Enerfly is a butterfly Yo-kai who brings people to their peak condition. That sounds like it would help you in battle . . . until you realize that Enerfly is constantly bringing *himself* to peak condition, too. Just don't confuse him with Enefly. That gets his wings all bent out of shape!

STATS

Tribe: Heartful

Attack: Slap

Soultimate Move: Energy Heaven

Favorite Food: Juice

Secret Weapon: Energy drinks

Inspirit: Energize

Easiness to Befriend: ★ ★ ★ ★

THE SHOWDOWN

So alike, yet so different. Enerfly and Enefly are nearly identical—except that their inspiriting powers have the exact opposite effect. One makes friendships, the other breaks friendships. Who will win?

HEARTFUL

STATS

Tribe: Heartful

Attack: Slap

Soultimate Move: Enemy Aura

Favorite Food: Juice

Secret Weapon: Breakup letters

Inspirit: Enemy Maker

Easiness to Befriend: ★★★★

ENEFLY

Enefly is also a butterfly Yo-kai. But unlike Enerfly, who makes people better, Enefly makes people cut ties with their best friends. He uses his opponents' emotions to his advantage in battle. Just don't confuse him with Enerfly. That gets his wings all—well, you know.

B3-NK1 VS. BEETLER

BRAVE

STATS

B3-NK1

B3-NK1 may very well be the world's first cyborg Yo-kai. His body is half machine, and he can use his pole arm to pierce through technological devices and assimilate them as part of his own "ultimate weapon." Talk about an upgrade!

Tribe: Brave
Attack: Lightning Slash
Soultimate Move: B3-NK1 Gun
Favorite Food: Chinese food
Secret Weapon: Hardware upgrades
Inspirit: Cyborg Strength
Easiness to Befriend: ★ ★

THE SHOWDOWN

Both B3-NK1 and Beetler are brave warriors. One is a cyborg and the other is a beetle . . . thing. Whatever the outcome, this match is certainly a sight to behold!

BRAVE

STATS

Tribe: Brave

Attack: One-Two Punch

Soultimate Move: Big Pincers

Favorite Food: Vegetables

Secret Weapon: Bugging people

Inspirit: Stag Power

Easiness to Befriend: ★ ★ ★

BEETLER

This young fighter may look like a harmless beetle, but don't be fooled. He has the heart of a warrior and a super tough pincer grip! Beetler fights with his horns as well as his fists, and he likes to knock his opponents flat with a one-two punch.

Q MYSTERIOUS

STATS

WAZZAT

Munch, munch, munch. Waz-zat sound? It's just Wazzat munching on your mind! This Yo-kai feeds off people's memories and makes them forget things. He's helpful when you want someone to forget an embarrassing story. He's less helpful when he makes you forget your own attack strategy!

Tribe: Mysterious

Attack: Bite

Soultimate Move: Wuwuzzat?

Favorite Food: Candy

Secret Weapon: His fashion sense. (He is a stylish headpiece, after all.)

Inspirit: Memory Eater

Easiness to Befriend: ★★★★★

THE SHOWDOWN

Wazzat tries to chow down on Daiz's memories, but no one knows if there are any memories there to begin with. Waz-a-hat to do?

SLIPPERY

STATS

Tribe: Slippery

Attack: Body Bash

Soultimate Move: Spacing Out

Favorite Food: Candy

Secret Weapon: Deep thoughts

Inspirit: Generous Heart

Easiness to Befriend: ★★★

DAIZ

Daiz is a very strange Yo-kai. He doesn't do much. In fact, he just stares off into space. Sometimes for three whole days. What is he thinking about all that time?

HEHEHEEL VS. COMPUNZER

SLIPPERY

HEHEHEEL

This eel just can't stop laughing, and nobody knows why. Maybe his sense of humor is broken. But he'll make the people he inspirits laugh along with him—whether something's funny or not. It can be hard to win a fight when you're rolling on the ground with laughter.

STATS

Tribe: Slippery
Attack: Chomp
Soultimate Move: In Da Funny Bone
Favorite Food: Meat
Secret Weapon: Quirky sense of humor
Inspirit: Playfulness
Easiness to Befriend: ★ ★ ★

THE SHOWDOWN

It's the ultimate jokester versus the ultimate laugher. One tells jokes that aren't funny, but the other thinks everything is hysterical. Who will have the last laugh?

EERIE

STATS

Tribe: Eerie

Attack: Beat

Soultimate Move: Lamest Joke

Favorite Food: Chinese food

Secret Weapon: Ability to laugh at himself

Inspirit: Fall Flat

Easiness to Befriend: ★ ★ ★

COMPUNZER

Knock, knock? Who's there? It's Compunzer with a bad joke. (*Wah, wah.*) Even though he wants to make people laugh, this Yo-kai's shtick just falls flat. It's a tough night at the microphone when a stand-up comic and Compunzer cross paths.

BUHU VS. DISMARELDA

EERIE

STATS

BUHU

Buhu is the perfect Yo-kai to build your hopes up before smashing them to bits. She brings bad luck and disappointment wherever she goes by making people think something good is about to happen. Then she pulls the rug out from under them. Talk about a spoilsport!

Tribe: Eerie

Attack: Pesky Pole

Soultimate Move: Boo Hoo Blast

Favorite Food: Bread

Secret Weapon: Sob story

Inspirit: Depression

Easiness to Befriend: ★ ★ ★ ★ ★

THE SHOWDOWN

Who will win in the battle of doom versus gloom? Dismarelda makes Buhu feel even grumpier than usual. But is Buhu just giving Dismarelda a false sense of victory before taking home the prize?

EERIE

STATS

Tribe: Eerie

Attack: Squish

Soultimate Move: Dismartillery

Favorite Food: Bread

Secret Weapon: Misery loves company #nofilter

Inspirit: Overcast

Easiness to Befriend: ★★★★

DISMARELDA

Feeling down? Dismarelda must be around. This big, blobby Yo-kai causes discord wherever she goes. The good news? She's married to Happierre, so the two cancel each other out. The bad news? That won't help in battle when Dismarelda uses her gloomy ways to her advantage.

DANDOODLE VS. SHMOOPIE

EERIE

DANDOODLE

Dandoodle is technically a Manjimutt, but through some sort of mistake he became incredibly handsome. He has a perfectly chiseled face, an adorable poodle body, and oh, that smile. Dogs love him. Women can't resist him. And he can turn things around him handsome, too! *Wonderful.*

STATS

Tribe: Eerie

Attack: Tackle

Soultimate Move: Handsome Grin

Favorite Food: Chinese food

Secret Weapon: His smile is so soothing

Inspirit: Healing Air

Easiness to Befriend: Unknown

THE SHOWDOWN

Shmoopie is literally All. The. Cuteness. But Dandoodle is, well, Dandoodle. The explosion of adorable from this matchup may just unravel the fabric of reality itself.

CHARMING

STATS

Tribe: Charming

Attack: Bite

Soultimate Move: Heartstring Tug

Favorite Food: Hamburger

Secret Weapon: Puppy-dog eyes

Inspirit: Skip a Beat

Easiness to Befriend: ★★★★

SHMOOPIE

Shmoopie is cute enough to melt anyone's heart . . . and he knows it. This puppy Yo-kai can be quite the schemer, so watch out! Shmoopie makes people pull an adorable face so no one gets mad at them, but turning all your opponents all goopy is no way to win a battle.

CHEEKSQUEEK VS. FIDGEPHANT

EERIE

CHEEKSQUEEK

Stinky doesn't begin to cut it when it comes to Cheeksqueek's cheese-cutting capabilities. This foul-smelling Yo-kai makes people fart unexpectedly and at the worst possible times. He may not be the most powerful fighter, but he can clear a room faster than you can say *toot*.

STATS

Tribe: Eerie

Attack: Headbutt

Soultimate Move: Stinky Smog

Favorite Food: Milk

Secret Weapon: Beans

Inspirit: Stink Up

Easiness to Befriend: ★ ★ ★ ★ ★

THE SHOWDOWN

It's Number 1 versus Number 2. Fidgephant puts the pressure on Cheeksqueek, but the gassy Yo-kai can make Fidgephant fidget from both ends. Who will burst first?

TOUGH

STATS

Tribe: Tough

Attack: Full swing

Soultimate Move: Fidgeting Smack

Favorite Food: Rice balls

Secret Weapon: Running water

Inspirit: Fidgeting

Easiness to Befriend: ★★★★

FIDGEPHANT

What's worse than having to battle a Yo-kai? Well, how about having to run to the bathroom while battling a Yo-kai? Fidgephant makes his opponents have to, um, go. As in answer the call of nature, or "see a man about a horse." Talk about pressure!

❤️ **CHARMING**

SWELTERRIER

Swelterrier makes you feel the heat during a matchup. His fiery heart and body always keep him burning hot. But don't sweat it. Deep down, this little guy just wants to cool off.

STATS

Tribe: Charming
Attack: Ventilator
Soultimate Move: Heat Wave
Favorite Food: Ramen
Secret Weapon: Preheating for battle
Inspirit: Blazing Heart
Easiness to Befriend: ★★

THE SHOWDOWN

Fire versus water, round two. Swelterrier puts the heat on Supyo, but the bodacious kappa isn't getting steamed anytime soon. Who will win?

CHARMING

STATS

Tribe: Charming

Attack: Double Slice

Soultimate Move: Bodacious Slash

Favorite Food: Vegetables

Secret Weapon: Pickup lines

Inspirit: Surf Power

Easiness to Befriend: ★★

SUPYO

Supyo isn't your ordinary kappa. Rather than sticking to the river, Supyo likes to live life on the edge, surfing and picking up girls. He'll put all his spirit into his water blade to defeat opponents in battle quickly. Then he gets back to catching waves.

NOWAY VS. BLOWKADE

TOUGH

STATS

NOWAY

Noway has a way of turning your life upside down. Want to go to a party? *No way.* Want that big promotion? *No way.* That's how Noway rolls—he makes people say "no" to things they really want to do. Will he let you beat him in battle? You know the answer.

Tribe: Tough

Attack: Body Bash

Soultimate Move: No Way Through

Favorite Food: Ramen

Secret Weapon: Absolute commitment to two-word answers

Inspirit: Refusal

Easiness to Befriend: ★★★★

THE SHOWDOWN

Nothing gets past these two, but waiting for one of them to make a move may take quite a while. It's a showdown of stubbornness that may just go nowhere.

TOUGH

STATS

Tribe: Tough

Attack: Palm Strike

Soultimate Move: Barricade Block

Favorite Food: Milk

Secret Weapon: Tight spaces

Inspirit: Needle Poke

Easiness to Befriend: ★★★★

BLOWKADE

Blowkade is one weird Yo-kai. He's half blowfish, half boulder, and all kinds of stubborn. Blowkade likes to block people's paths for no particular reason. He doesn't really want to battle you. He just doesn't want you to get where you're going.

DRAGGIE VS. SNOTSOLONG

SLIPPERY

DRAGGIE

This runny-nosed dragon is just a tiny tyke who wants attention. But the crystal ball on his head is far more powerful than you'd think. It can reveal the future and even see the hidden strengths of his opponents.

STATS

Tribe: Slippery
Attack: Headsmack
Soultimate Move: Draggie Stone
Favorite Food: Chinese food
Secret Weapon: The gift of foresight
Inspirit: Dragon Power
Easiness to Befriend: ★ ★ ★

THE SHOWDOWN

Someone give these two Yo-kai a box of tissues! Both Draggie and Snotsolong have constantly runny noses. First to slip on the other's snot will lose the showdown!

9

MYSTERIOUS

STATS

Tribe: Mysterious

Attack: Pesky Poke

Soultimate Move: Stretchy Slap

Favorite Food: Seafood

Secret Weapon: LOTS of tissues

Inspirit: Runny Nose

Easiness to Befriend: ★★★★★

SNOTSOLONG

Poor Snotsolong suffers from an insanely runny nose, and he makes anyone he inspirits share the same fate. He may be annoying, but you have to feel for him. Secretly, Snotsolong is scared the snot from his runny nose will make him too heavy to fly.

VENOCT VS. DRAGON LORD

SLIPPERY

VENOCT

The elite Yo-kai Venoct has an incredible amount of power. He can break the ground by punching it and he uses his living dragon scarf as a weapon. Venoct was once a little boy whose village was destroyed by a vicious Yo-kai. Now he's on a quest for revenge—and will defeat anyone who stands in his way.

STATS

Tribe: Slippery

Attack: Maul

Soultimate Move: Octo Snake

Favorite Food: Seafood

Secret Weapon: Fashion-forward neckwear

Inspirit: Venoct's Blessing

Easiness to Befriend: Unknown

THE SHOWDOWN

The sheer power of this matchup is earth-shattering. Both Venoct and Dragon Lord fight with honor. But which master will prove victorious?

SLIPPERY

STATS

Tribe: Slippery

Attack: Maul

Soultimate Move: Dragon Rock

Favorite Food: Chinese food

Secret Weapon: He's the stuff of legends

Inspirit: Dragon Power

Easiness to Befriend: ★ ★

DRAGON LORD

The evolved version of Draggie, Dragon Lord has really come into his own. He has dignity and might worthy of the title "dragon." His strength is first rate, and since he's armed with a crystal ball that can show his opponent's next move, he's nearly unstoppable.

SHEEN VS. REUKNIGHT

BRAVE

STATS

Tribe: Brave
Attack: Lightning Slash
Soultimate Move: Legendary Slash
Favorite Food: Seafood
Secret Weapon: Sharp things
Inspirit: Fine Weapon
Easiness to Befriend: ★★

SHEEN

When the fabled Legend Blade fused with the gambling Yo-kai Chansin, Sheen's mighty spirit was reignited! This swordsman is a martial arts master who battles with the power of wind and lightning on his side. He's truly a force to be reckoned with.

THE SHOWDOWN

Both Sheen and Reuknight are motivated warriors, but only one can win. Will swords or spears triumph in this battle of the masters?

BRAVE

STATS

Tribe: Brave

Attack: Stab Storm

Soultimate Move: Knight's Slash

Favorite Food: Vegetables

Secret Weapon: Epic tales of glory

Inspirit: Knight's Curse

Easiness to Befriend: ★★

REUKNIGHT

A noble knight if ever there was one, Reuknight is the combined version of Helmsman and Armsman. Now whole again, Reuknight aspires to do what he couldn't when he was alive—unify the country. He desires not to fight you, good Yo-kai. But take heed, he will if he must.

ROBONYAN VS. SHOGUNYAN

TOUGH

ROBONYAN

Robonyan is a robotic version of Jibanyan from the future. Or at least, he says he is. Either way, he's one tough kitty! From rocket punches to a personal chocobar factory inside his body, this souped-up Jibanyan has got it going on.

STATS

Tribe: Tough

Attack: Rocket Punch

Soultimate Move: Guard Meowde

Favorite Food: Seafood

Secret Weapon: He's from the future. Everything is better in the future.

Inspirit: Steel Power

Easiness to Befriend: ★★

THE SHOWDOWN

Jibanyan's ancestor and future self go head-to-head in this matchup! It's samurai-kitty versus robo-cat. To the victor go the chocobars! Let the battle begin!

BRAVE

STATS

Tribe: Brave

Attack: Lightning Slash

Soultimate Move: Bonito Blade

Favorite Food: Seafood & Skipjack tuna

Secret Weapon: Travel-sized sword sharpener

Inspirit: Heart of a Warrior

Easiness to Befriend: Unknown

SHOGUNYAN

The spirit of Jibanyan's ancestor, Shogunyan is a legendary Yo-kai. Not much is known about him except that he is an adorable samurai sword master. His slashing skills serve him well during battle and when slicing equally sized pieces of cake.

THE YO-KAI EXPERTS' PICKS

PGS. 4-5: JIBANYAN VS. MANJIMUTT
WINNER: JIBANYAN
Not much of a match, as Jibanyan easily overwhelms Manjimutt with his Paws of Fury.

PGS. 6-7: BLAZION VS. WALKAPPA
WINNER: BLAZION
Walkappa tries to spread the love, but in the end, Blazion's quick thinking helps him win. Walkappa's plate, his source of energy, is quickly dried out, and he is unable to continue.

PGS. 8-9: ROUGHRAFF VS. HAPPIERRE
WINNER: HAPPIERRE
Roughraff may look tough, but he's no match for Happierre, who overwhelms the renegade Yo-kai with positive vibes.

PGS. 10-11: KOMASAN VS. KOMAJIRO
WINNER: KOMAJIRO
Though they have almost the same stats, Komajiro takes the win with his resourcefulness. But don't worry, these country boys are still the best of brothers!

PGS. 12-13: TATTLETELL VS. HIDABAT
WINNER: HIDABAT
Hidabat shows Tattletell that when you have no friends, there aren't many secrets to tell.

PGS. 14-15: BLIZZARIA VS. EVERFORE
WINNER: BLIZZARIA
Blizzaria proves that the power of the elements can sometimes be stronger than the desire for beauty.

PGS. 16-17: INSOMNI VS. WIGLIN
WINNER: INSOMNI
Even a dancing seaweed needs downtime to reenergize. Insomni shows Wiglin that you really can stop the beat, especially when you need sleep.

PGS. 18-19: KYUBI VS. CASANUVA
WINNER: KYUBI
Kyubi's fire power is overwhelming, but with all those girls fawning over Casanuva, you have to wonder who the real winner is ...

PGS. 20-21: SIGNIBBLE VS. CHATALIE
WINNER: SIGNIBBLE
These two are pretty evenly matched, but there's only so much showing off you can do when your cell phone is out of batteries.

PGS. 22-23: ENERFLY VS. ENEFLY
WINNER: ENEFLY
Being nearly identical counterparts, this match is incredibly close. In the end, Enefly's slight advantage in strength proves to be the deciding factor.

PGS. 24-25: B3-NK1 VS. BEETLER
WINNER: BEETLER
B3-NK1 may have technology on his side, but in the end, Beetler lands a final strike that shuts down B3-NK1's operating system.

PGS. 26-27: WAZZAT VS. DAIZ
WINNER: DAIZ
Wazzat tries to defeat Daiz with his memory-munching skills, but can't quite seem to get a good bite. How can you forget something you never remembered?

PGS. 28-29: HEHEHEEL VS. COMPUNZER
WINNER: COMPUNZER
Compunzer's bad jokes turn out to be too much for Heheheel and leave him ROFL.

PGS. 30-31: BUHU VS. DISMARELDA
WINNER: BUHU
Dismarelda seemed guaranteed to win, but Buhu causes a little too much bad luck for Dismarelda to handle. Boo-hoo ...

PGS. 32-33: DANDOODLE VS. SHMOOPIE
WINNER: DANDOODLE
Dandoodle overwhelms his competition in skill, technique, strength, and handsome looks. However, Shmoopie's innocent puppy face guarantees a gentle pampering after the showdown.

PGS. 34-35: CHEEKSQUEEK VS. FIDGEPHANT
WINNER: CHEEKSQUEEK
Poor Fidgephant ends up being overwhelmed by everything, making it an easy victory for Cheeksqueek.

PGS. 36-37: SWELTERRIER VS. SUPYO
WINNER: SUPYO
This kappa sure has gotten stronger since his water-carrying days! Supyo utilizes his elemental powers to cool down Swelterrier and get the win.

PGS. 38-39: NOWAY VS. BLOWKADE
WINNER: BLOWKADE
In the end, Blowkade shows Noway the importance of putting strength behind your words.

PGS. 40-41: DRAGGIE VS. SNOTSOLONG
WINNER: DRAGGIE
It's a surprise they didn't get caught in each other's snot and end up with a tie! But Draggie looks into his crystal ball and sees Snotsolong's Stretchy Slap ahead of time and dodges the attack for the win.

PGS. 42-43: VENOCT VS. DRAGON LORD
WINNER: DRAGON LORD
Try as he might, Venoct is unable to overcome Dragon Lord's formidable strength. Although he loses, Venoct vows to defeat his opponent in a highly anticipated rematch.

PGS. 44-45: SHEEN VS. REUKNIGHT
WINNER: SHEEN
Swords wind up overpowering spears in this heated battle. At the end of it all, Sheen and Reuknight find great respect for each other.

PGS. 46-47: ROBONYAN VS. SHOGUNYAN
WINNER: ROBONYAN
It's a close match, but luckily for Robonyan, his upgrades are good enough to defeat his legendary ancestor.